The Adventures of Dele the Street Kid

of Dele the Street Kid

Every Superhero Needs a Sidekick

Tomi Adetayo

illustrated by Tanja Russita

a1000faces
different faces: fascinating lives
#iam

ISBN: 978-1-7391729-2-3 (print)

978-1-7391729-1-6 (digital)

Cover design by Tanja Russita

Editing by Trisha Crabtree and Bryony van der Merwe

Printed in the United Kingdom

First Edition printed in 2023

For more information,

contact the author at project@a1000faces.com

www.a1000faces.com/books

For Obafemi and Omotara,
Always let your light shine.

To each child in the world.

You can become **anything** you set your mind to.

Go ahead and don't stop.

Under an old wobbly bridge rests a boy named Dele. He is alone, curled up under his special blanket. Dele imagines himself as a **SUPERHERO** in the night sky, flying through puffy clouds and touching ice crystals.

Before falling asleep, Dele counts the twinkling stars. There are so many! He wishes he could share these moments with *someone.*

Dele wakes in the morning to the sound of cars rushing by

—vroom vroom—

and people bustling about.

He yawns.

"Time to sell Mr Odu's bread!"

On the way to work, Dele pretends to be a superhero
as he runs, skips and tumbles along the busy roads.

"Wheeeeeeee! I can fly!

Watch me

goooooooooo!"

"Good morning, Dele," Mr Odu says.
"Can you count how many rolls you must sell today?"

Dele counts each roll. "1, 2, 3, 4, 5."

"Well done

and be careful!" says Mr Odu.

Dele balances the tray on his head and daydreams about being a superhero. Wouldn't it be wonderful, he thinks, to have a sidekick flying alongside him?

Every

SUPERHERO

has one.

As Dele skips to a fruit stall, he hears a whimper.

Then another, **LOUDER** this time.

Dele decides to investigate.

Using his superhero vision,

he spots **three** children teasing a street dog.

"OH NO!

I should help that poor dog, but I'm alone,"

Dele thinks.

"If I had a sidekick,
we could save the day
together."

The dog yelps,

and even though he has no sidekick,

Dele **knows** what he **must** do.

Dele puts on his superhero face.

He stands tall, **puffs out his chest,**

and gives the loudest shout he can muster.

"Aaaaaaah!

Leave that dog **alone!**"

Alarmed by Dele's outburst, the children run away.

Dele jumps high. "**Woo-hoo!** I did it! I'm a

SUPERHERO!"

Dele continues selling Mr Odu's rolls and,

as the sun sets, he returns to the bakery with

an **empty** tray.

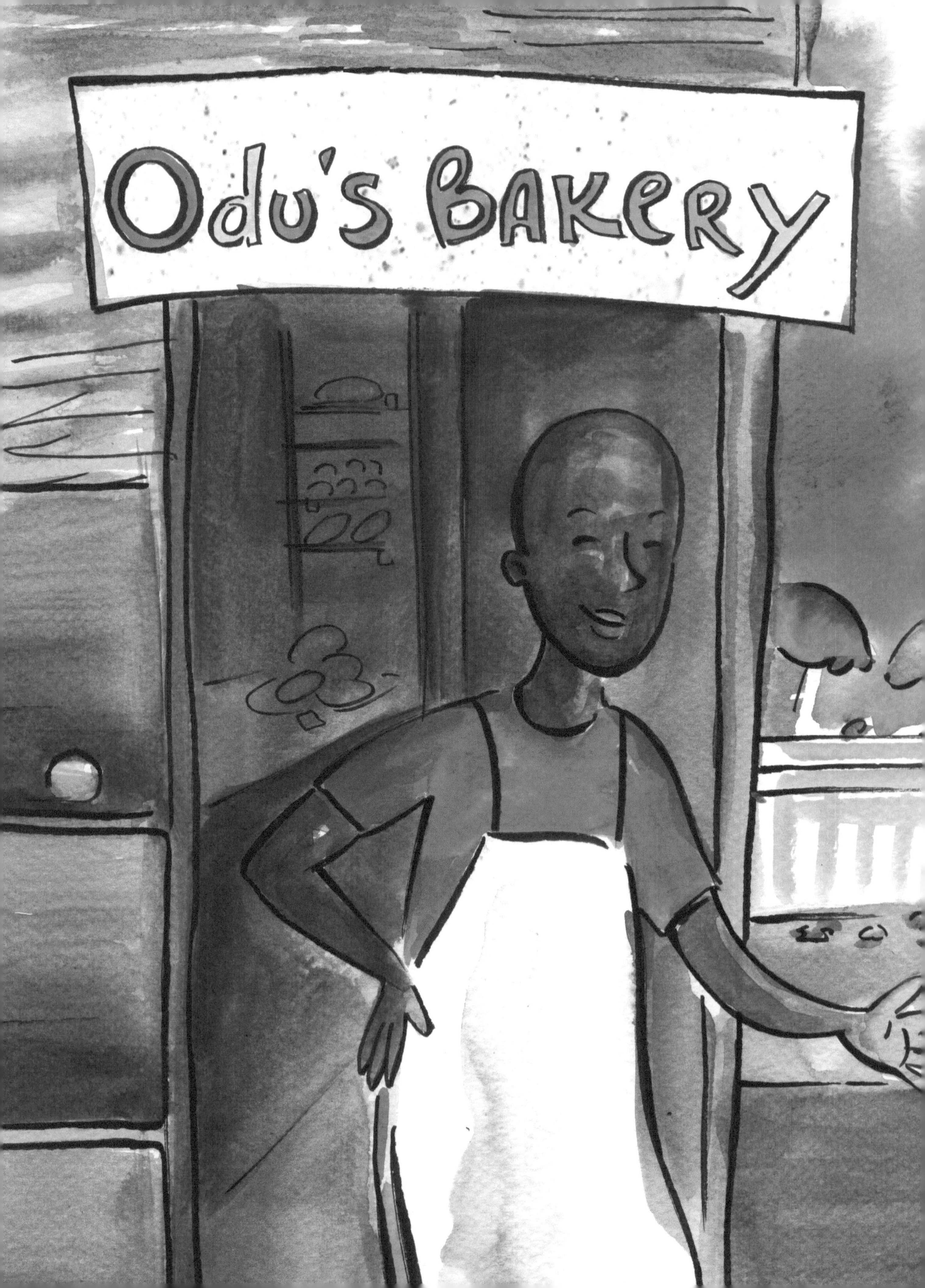
Odu's BAKERY

"**Well done,**" Mr Odu says, paying Dele.

"You sold **everything** again today."

"THANK YOU,"

says Dele smiling.

When it's nearly bedtime, Dele waves to the other street children and settles beneath the old **wobbly** bridge. He doesn't count the stars tonight. Instead, he thinks about his **SUPERHERO** feat.

Dele is **proud** to have **saved** the poor dog.

Dele has an idea.

"Maybe that dog needs a

friend!"

It's late, but Dele has a new SUPERHERO mission.
He searches for the dog in the darkening streets.
After a while, Dele wants to give up, but he doesn't because

SUPERHEROES
NEVER GIVE UP.

Dele finally spots the dog. "I'm Dele. I **rescued** you today."

The dog whimpers. Dele sits beside him and strokes him.

"**Don't worry;** you can stay

with me."

The dog wags his tail and follows Dele.

"I will call you Timi.

You can be my SIDEKICK."

Together, they sit beneath the old wobbly bridge and watch the twinkling lights in the sky.

"Someday, Timi,"

Dele says,

"we will fly together."